More Folk Stories

A Dolch Classic Basic Reading Book

by Edward W. Dolch and Marguerite P. Dolch

illustrated by Kersti Frigell

The Basic Reading Books

The Basic Reading Books are fun reading books that fill the need for easy-to-read stories for the primary grades. The interest appeal of these folktales and legends will encourage independent reading at the early reading levels.

The stories focus on the 95 Common Nouns and the Dolch 220 Basic Sight Vocabulary. Beyond these simple lists, the books use about two or three new words per page.

This series was prepared under the direction and supervision of Edward W. Dolch, Ph.D.

This revision was prepared under the direction and supervision of Eleanor Dolch LaRoy and the Dolch Family Trust.

SRA/McGraw-Hill

*A Division of The **McGraw·Hill** Companies*

Printed in the United States of America.

Send all inquiries to:
SRA/McGraw-Hill
250 Old Wilson Bridge Road, Suite 310
Worthington, OH 43085

ISBN 0-02-830815-8

1 2 3 4 5 6 7 8 9 0 BUX 04 03 02 01 00 99 98

Table of Contents

The Little Red Hen and the Fox 5

The Cap That Mother Made 11

The Gingerbread Boy 18

Aiken-Drum 23

The Rabbit Who Was Afraid 29

Silly Jack 35

The Three Little Pigs 41

The Bear That Liked Music 52

The Coldest Time of the Year 56

The Little Red Hen and the Fox

Once upon a time a little, red hen lived in a house upon a hill. And far down the hill, under a big, big stone lived a fox and his mother.

One day the fox said to his mother, "I would like a chicken to eat."

"The little, red hen lives up on the hill," said his mother. "She would be very good to eat."

The fox laughed and said, "Mother, put the pot on the fire, and fill it full of water. I am going up the hill to get the little, red hen."

And the fox went up the hill with a big bag to get the little, red hen.

The little, red hen had on her blue
apron. She was cleaning her house. She
had all the doors and windows opened.
When the fox got to her little house, he
walked right in the door.

"Good morning, Little Red Hen,"
said the fox. "I have come up the hill to
see you."

The little, red hen did not know what to do. She did not like the fox, because she knew that the fox liked to eat chickens. But she said, "Good morning, Mr. Fox. You must be tired after your long walk up the hill. Will you sit down by the fire?"

The fox sat down in the big chair. And the little, red hen went out to get a stick of wood for the fire. When she came back, the fox looked as if he were sleeping. But when the little, red hen went to put the stick of wood on the fire, the fox jumped up. He put a bag right over the little, red hen. He took a string out of his pocket and put it around and around the top of the bag.

"Now, I will have a little, red hen to eat," laughed the fox. And he put the bag on his back and started down the hill.

It was a long, long way down the hill. Soon the fox was very tired. He sat down under a tree and he put the bag down on the grass. Then the fox went to sleep.

The little, red hen had been thinking and thinking. She had to get out of that bag. Now the little, red hen had some scissors in the pocket of her blue apron. When the fox put the bag on the grass, she took her scissors out of her pocket and cut the bag. Then Little Red Hen got out of the bag.

She looked all around. She saw a stone as big as she was. She put the stone in the bag. She took some of the string from around the top of the bag and sewed up the bag where she had cut it.

Then the little, red hen ran up the hill to her house as fast as she could go.

Pretty soon the fox opened his eyes. "My, my," said the fox to himself, "I must take this chicken to my mother. She will be wanting to eat it."

The fox got up and put the bag on his back and went down the hill to his house.

"Did you bring me the little, red hen?" asked his mother.

"She is here in the bag," said the fox. "Do you have the pot of hot water to put her in?"

"Yes," said the mother, "let us put the little, red hen into the pot of hot water."

"I will hold the bag," said the fox. "You take the string off of the top of the bag. Then we will both put the little, red hen into the pot."

But into the pot went, not the little, red hen, but the big stone. And the hot water went all over the fox and his mother.

Oh, how they ran around and around! And never again did that fox go up the hill to get the little, red hen.

The Cap That Mother Made

There was once a little boy called Andrew. One day his mother made him a new, red cap. It was the prettiest cap that Andrew had ever seen. And it was his very own.

Everyone thought that Andrew looked very fine in his new, red cap. Andrew put on his new, red cap and went for a walk down the road.

As Andrew was going down the road, he saw a big boy.

"What a fine, red cap you have," said the big boy. "I will give you my cat if you will give me your red cap."

Now Andrew wanted a cat. But he could not give away the new, red cap that his mother had made.

"No, no," said Andrew, "I cannot give you my new, red cap." And Andrew walked on down the road.

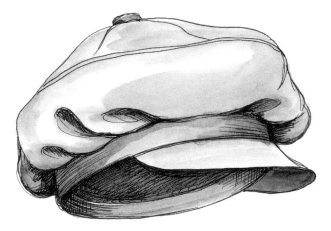

Before long, Andrew saw an old woman. The old woman called to Andrew: "Andrew, my boy, what a fine, red cap you have on your head."

"Yes," said Andrew. "My mother made it for me."

"And where are you going, Andrew, my boy, with that fine, red cap upon your head?" asked the old woman.

"I think," said Andrew, "that I will go to see the king. I want him to see my new,

red cap that my mother made for me."
And Andrew walked on down the road.

Pretty soon, Andrew got to the palace where the king lived. He was going to walk right in the door, but the soldiers by the door would not let him in.

"Who are you?" the soldiers said. "Why do you wish to go into the king's palace?"

"I am Andrew," said the little boy, "and I wish to show the king the new, red cap that my mother made for me."

But the soldiers only laughed and would not let him into the palace.

Just then the princess passed by. She saw the little boy at the door of the palace. "Who are you?" asked the princess.

"I am Andrew," said the little boy, "and I wish to show the king the new, red cap that my mother made for me."

"Come with me," said the princess, "and we will go and find the king."

So Andrew and the princess walked into the palace hand in hand. The palace was a big, big palace, and they walked and walked.

At last they got to a big room. And in the room was a long table. And at the head of the table sat the queen in a gold chair. And on the table were big, red apples and white cakes and many good things to eat.

"Mother," said the princess, "this is Andrew. He has come to show us his new, red cap."

"Come, Andrew," said the queen, "and sit on this chair by me."

Andrew sat down on a gold chair by the queen and the princess sat down on a gold chair by Andrew. The queen gave Andrew a big, red apple and some white cake.

"You will want to take your cap off when you eat," said the queen.

"Oh, no, no, no," said Andrew, "I can eat with my new, red cap upon my head." And Andrew put both hands on his red cap.

"I will give you this pretty ring if you will give me your red cap," said the princess. And she showed Andrew a very pretty ring that was on her hand.

Andrew thought the ring was very pretty. He would have liked to show the ring to his mother.

"No, no," said Andrew, "I cannot give you my new, red cap."

Just then the king came into the room.

"Father," said the princess, "this is Andrew, and he wants to show you his new, red cap."

The king looked at Andrew and he said, "Andrew, my boy, that is a very, very pretty red cap. I think that I would like to have that red cap on my own head. How would you like to put on my gold crown?"

Andrew thought that the king's gold crown was very pretty. He would have liked to show it to his mother, but he could not give away the red cap that his mother had made.

"No, no, no," said Andrew, "I cannot give you my new, red cap."

Andrew got down off of the gold chair. He ran out of the room. He ran out of the palace. And he ran home just as fast as he could go.

"Mother, mother!" cried Andrew. "The big boy said that he would give me his cat for my red cap. The princess said that she would give me her pretty ring for my red cap, and the king said that he would give me his gold crown for my red cap. But I would not give my red cap away, because you made this red cap just for me."

The Gingerbread Boy

Once there was a little, old woman and a little, old man. They lived in a pretty, little house. But no little boy lived with them. And no little girl lived with them. One day the little, old woman said, "I will make a Gingerbread Boy." And that is just what she did.

The little, old woman cut a boy out of gingerbread. She made him a cap and a coat out of gingerbread. She made him two eyes and a nose. Oh, my, what a pretty-looking Gingerbread Boy he was! Then the old woman put him into the oven to bake.

Pretty soon the little, old woman opened the oven door and looked into the oven. She wanted to see if the Gingerbread Boy was done.

"Let me out of here! Let me out of here!" said the Gingerbread Boy, and he jumped out of the oven.

"I am a little gingerbread boy. I am, I am. I can run away from you. I can, I can."

The little gingerbread boy ran out of the door. And the little, old woman ran after him. But she could not catch him.

The little, old man was working in the garden. The gingerbread boy called to him as he ran, "I am a little gingerbread boy. I am, I am. I ran away from the little, old woman. I can run away from you. I can, I can."

The little, old man ran after the gingerbread boy. But he could not catch him.

The little gingerbread boy ran down the road. Soon he saw a brown-and-white cow eating the green grass. He called to the cow, "I am a little gingerbread boy. I am, I am. I ran away from the little, old woman. I ran away from the little, old man. I can run away from you. I can, I can."

The brown-and-white cow ran after the gingerbread boy. But she could not catch him.

The little gingerbread boy ran faster and faster. Pretty soon, he saw a black-and-white pig eating corn and he called, "I am a little gingerbread boy. I am, I am. I ran away from the little, old woman. I ran away from the little, old man.

I ran away from the brown-and-white cow. I can run away from you. I can, I can."

The pig stopped eating the yellow corn. He ran after the gingerbread boy. But he could not catch him.

"No one can catch me," laughed the gingerbread boy. And he ran away as fast as he could go.

Soon the gingerbread boy saw an old, red fox. He called to the fox, "I am a little gingerbread boy. I am, I am. I ran away from the little, old woman. I ran

away from the little, old man. I ran away from the brown-and-white cow. I ran away from the black-and-white pig. I can run away from you. I can, I can."

But the old, red fox just went to sleep. He did not run after the gingerbread boy.

The little gingerbread boy stopped and called to the fox, "You cannot catch me."

The old, red fox just opened one eye and said, "What did you say? I cannot hear you."

The little gingerbread boy went right up to the fox.

The fox opened both his eyes. He gave one jump, and he ate the gingerbread boy all up.

"Oh dear, oh dear!" said the gingerbread boy. "Now I am all gone."

Aiken-Drum

Once there was a town by a woods, far, far away. The men and the women and the children who lived in this town worked very hard, but they could never get all the work done.

One day, just as the sun was going down some men were talking together. One man said, "I will never get all my corn into the barn before the snow comes."

Another man said, "You all like the bread that I bake. Every day someone comes to my store for bread, but I have run out. I must have someone to help me bake more bread."

And another man said, "I have too many cows to milk. I need someone to help me milk the cows."

And as the men were talking, they could hear someone singing, "Have you any work for Aiken-Drum? Any work for Aiken-Drum?"

They looked down the street, but they did not see anyone. However, they could hear someone singing, "Have you any work for Aiken-Drum? Any work for Aiken-Drum?"

The women and the children came out of the houses. "We hear someone singing," they said. And they looked down the street.

Then a little girl cried, "Look, look! I see a funny, little man coming down the street."

Then the men and the women were all afraid, because they could see no one.

"He is only as big as we are," said one of the little children.

"His eyes are so big and round and black," said another.

"Is he going to hurt us?" asked one of the children.

And then an old, old grandmother came to see why everyone was looking down the street. She, too, could hear the singing, "Have you any work for Aiken-Drum? Any work for Aiken-Drum?"

"It is a brownie," said the old grandmother. "Many a time when I was little, my mother told me about the brownies. They are good little people that love to work. Be good to this brownie, and he will help you."

And that is how the brownie named Aiken-Drum came to live in that far, far away town.

Every day the old, old grandmother put out some bread and some milk for the brownie. But only the children could see him.

Aiken-Drum worked and worked, because he loved to work. He worked for all the men and women and children in the town. He milked the cows. He got the yellow corn into the barn. He baked the bread. He made the beds and cleaned the houses. And when no grownup was around, he would play with the children and sing to them.

Now there was a good man of the
town who said to his wife, "Aiken-Drum
has been very good to us. He has helped
us with our work. I think that we should
do something for him."

"I would like to make him a new
coat and a new cap," said the wife. And
that is just what the good woman did.
She made Aiken-Drum a little, brown
coat and a little, green cap. The good
man put the little, brown coat and the

little, green hat by the bread and milk that the grandmother put out for the brownie.

The good man and the good woman forgot what the old, old grandmother had once told them. "A brownie works because he loves to work. You must never give a brownie anything."

Aiken-Drum found the little brown coat and the little green cap. He knew they were for him.

"Oh, oh, oh!" cried Aiken-Drum. "What a pretty little coat. What a pretty little cap. But now I must go away."

Aiken-Drum went away.

But the children were always looking for Aiken-Drum. Every day they put bread and milk out for Aiken-Drum. But they never saw Aiken-Drum again.

The Rabbit Who Was Afraid

Once there was a little rabbit who was afraid of everything. He was afraid of the wind and the rain. But most of all, he was afraid that the earth would break up.

"What shall I do when the earth breaks up?" cried the little rabbit. And the big rabbits always laughed at him.

One day the little rabbit was sleeping under a coconut tree. There was

a monkey up in the coconut tree. The monkey thought that he would play a joke on the little rabbit. So he dropped a big coconut just behind the little rabbit.

The little rabbit jumped up. "Oh, oh, oh!" he cried. "The earth is breaking up. The earth is breaking up. What shall I do?"

The little rabbit jumped and ran as fast as he could. He did not look back. He just ran and ran.

The little rabbit saw some big rabbits and he cried, "The earth is breaking up! The earth is breaking up!"

The little rabbit was running so fast that the big rabbits ran after him.

Soon all the rabbits were running away together.

A deer saw the rabbits running. "Why are you running away so fast?" called the deer.

"The earth is breaking up!" cried the rabbits. "Come with us."

And the deer ran with the rabbits.

A fox saw them running. "Why are you running away so fast?" called the fox.

"The earth is breaking up!" cried the deer.

And so the fox ran with the deer and the rabbits. On and on they ran.

An elephant saw them running. "Why are you running away so fast?" called the elephant.

"The earth is breaking up!" cried the fox.

And so the elephant ran with the fox and the deer and the rabbits. They ran and ran and ran.

At last a lion saw them all running. "Why are you running away so fast?" called the lion.

"The earth is breaking up!" cried the elephant.

The lion looked around him. He did not see the earth breaking up. And so

the lion roared. He roared three times. The elephant and the fox and the deer and the rabbits stopped.

Lion said, "Elephant, you are the biggest. Why are you running away so fast?"

"Oh, King Lion," said the elephant, "the earth is breaking up."

"Who saw the earth breaking up?" asked the lion.

"I did not see it," said the fox. "The deer said that the earth was breaking up."

"I did not see it," said the deer. "The rabbits said that the earth was breaking up."

And the rabbits all looked at the little rabbit who was always afraid of everything.

"Little Rabbit," said the lion, "did you see the earth breaking up?"

"Oh, yes, King Lion," said the little rabbit. "I was asleep under a coconut tree. And the earth started to break up right there under the coconut tree. I ran away from there as fast I could go."

"Then," said the lion, "you and I will go back to the coconut tree where the earth started to break up."

So the lion put the little rabbit on his back and away they went.

They got to the coconut tree. The lion saw where the little rabbit had been sleeping. The lion saw the coconut in the grass. The lion saw the monkeys up in the coconut tree.

"Oh, Little Rabbit," said the lion, "the earth is not breaking up. It was only a coconut that had fallen from the tree."

And the monkeys up in the coconut tree laughed and laughed. They laughed at the joke they had played on the little rabbit who was afraid of everything.

Silly Jack

Once upon a time there was a boy
named Jack. He lived with his mother.
His mother worked hard all of the time,
but Jack was so silly that he did not
work at all. All Jack did was play in the
sun or sit by the fire and sleep.

One day his mother said, "Jack, you must go to work. If you want to eat, you must work."

And the day after that day, Jack went to work for a farmer.

And when the day was over, the farmer gave Jack some money. Jack had never had any money before, and he wanted to show it to his mother.

Jack went down the road, carrying the money in his hand. Before long, he lost the money. And when he got home and told his mother about the money, she said, "Jack, Jack, you lost the money because you carried it in your hand. You must carry things in your pocket."

"Carry it in my pocket," said Jack. "That is what I shall do."

And the day after that day, Jack went to help the farmer with his cows. And when the day was over, the farmer gave Jack some milk to take home.

Jack put the milk into his pocket and went down the road. And when he got home, the milk was gone.

"Oh, Jack," said his mother, "you lost the milk because you carried it in your pocket. You must carry milk in a pail on your head."

"Carry it on my head," said Jack. "That is just what I shall do."

And the day after that day, Jack went again to the farmer. And when the day was over, the farmer gave Jack some butter to take home.

And Jack went down the road carrying the butter on his head. And when he got home, the butter had run down all over his face and his coat.

"Jack, Jack," said his mother, "why did you carry the butter on your head? You must carry butter in your hands."

"Carry it in my hands," said Jack.
"That is just what I shall do."

The day after that day, Jack went to
work for a baker. And when the day was
over, the baker gave Jack a big, black cat
to take home.

Jack went down the road, carrying
the big, black cat in his hands. Pretty
soon, a dog ran up to them and the black
cat jumped out of Jack's hands.

"Oh, Jack," said his mother, "you lost the big, black cat because you carried her in your hands. You must put a string around a cat, and then she will walk with you down the road."

"Put a string around it. Put a string around it," said Jack. "That is just what I shall do."

And the day after that day, Jack went to work for a butcher. And when the day was over, the butcher gave Jack some meat to take home.

Jack put a string around the meat and went down the road pulling the meat by the string.

When he got home his mother said, "Jack, Jack, why did you pull that meat in the road? Now we cannot eat it. If you had carried the meat on your back, it would have been good to eat."

"Carry it on my back," said Jack. "That is just what I shall do."

And the day after that day, Jack went to work for a rich man. This rich man had a pretty daughter who had never laughed. And the rich man had said that anyone who could make his daughter laugh, could have a farm.

When the day was over, the rich man gave Jack a little donkey.

Do you know what Jack did? He put that donkey on his back.

The daughter of the rich man saw Jack going down the road with the donkey on his back. Jack looked so silly that she laughed and laughed.

The rich man gave Silly Jack a farm, and Jack was never silly again.

The Three Little Pigs

There was once an old mother pig who had three little pigs. One day the mother pig said, "Little pigs, the time has come for you to go out and make houses of your own."

The three little pigs said good-bye to their mother and went out to make their own houses.

The first little pig saw a man with some straw. The little pig said, "Please give me some straw so that I can make a house of my own."

"Yes," said the man, "I will give you some straw because you are a good little pig."

The first little pig made himself a house of the straw. And in no time at all, he had his house done.

The second little pig saw a man with some sticks. The little pig said, "Please

give me some sticks so that I can make a
house of my own."

"Yes," said the man, "I will give you
some sticks because you are a good little
pig."

The second little pig made himself a
house out of the sticks. And in no time at
all, he had his house done.

Now the third little pig saw a man with some bricks. The little pig said, "Please give me some bricks so that I can make a house of my own."

"Yes," said the man, "I will give you some bricks because you are a good little pig."

The third little pig worked a long time. He made himself a house out of bricks.

The first little pig lived in the house of straw. The second little pig lived in the house of sticks. And the third little pig lived in the house of bricks.

One day a wolf came by the house of straw. "My, my," said the wolf to himself, "I smell a little pig."

The wolf went up to the door of the house made of straw and said, "Little pig, little pig, let me in. Let me in."

But the first little pig said, "I know you, old wolf. You want to eat me. No, no, no, I will not let you in. Not by the hair of my chinny, chin, chin."

"Then I will huff and I will puff and I will blow your house in," said the old wolf.

So the old wolf huffed and he puffed, and he blew the house in. But the little pig ran out the back door. He ran as fast as he could to the second little pig that had the house of sticks.

And the old wolf did not get a little pig to eat that day.

One day the old wolf went by the house made of sticks. "My, my," said the old wolf to himself, "I smell two little pigs."

The old wolf went up to the door of the house made of sticks and said, "Little pigs, little pigs, let me in. Let me in."

But the two little pigs said, "We know you, old wolf. You want to eat us. No, no, no, we will not let you in. Not by the hair of our chinny, chin, chins."

"Then I will huff and I will puff and I will blow your house in." So the old wolf huffed and he puffed and he puffed

and he huffed and he blew the house down. But the two little pigs ran out the back door. They ran to the third little pig that had the house of bricks.

And the old wolf did not get two little pigs to eat that day.

One day the old wolf went by the house made of bricks. "My, my," said the old wolf to himself, "I smell three little pigs."

The old wolf went up to the door of the house made of bricks and said, "Little pigs, little pigs, let me in. Let me in."

But the three little pigs said, "No, no, no, we will not let you in. Not by the hair of our chinny, chin, chins."

"Then I will huff and I will puff, and I will blow your house in," said the old wolf. "I blew down the house of straw and I blew down the house of sticks."

He huffed and puffed. But he could not blow down the house of bricks. He could not hurt the three little pigs that lived in the house of bricks. The old wolf sat down to think.

Then the old wolf called to the little pigs, "Little pigs, little pigs, I know where there are some turnips."

Now the little pigs liked turnips very much. "We would like some turnips," said the three little pigs.

The wolf laughed to himself.

"Farmer Smith has some big, white turnips," said the old wolf. "In the morning I will come at six o'clock and show you where the turnips are."

But in the morning, the three little pigs got up at five o'clock. They went to Farmer Smith's farm. They got a basket of big, white turnips. Then they ran back to the little, brick house.

At six o'clock the old wolf came by. He went to the door and called:

"Little pigs, little pigs, let us go and get some turnips."

The little pigs said, "Go away, go away, old wolf. We have all the turnips that we want."

The old wolf sat down to think. "Turnips are very good," said the old wolf, "but I like red apples, too."

"And where are there red apples?" asked the three little pigs.

"Farmer Smith has some big, red apples on his farm," said the wolf. "In the morning, I will come at five o'clock and show you where the apples are."

The three little pigs liked to eat apples very much, and so they said: "Thank you, Mr. Wolf, for telling us about the apples. We would like some big red apples very much."

In the morning, the three little pigs got up at four o'clock and went to Farmer Smith's farm.

In the morning, the old wolf said to himself, "I think that those three little pigs are going to get up at four o'clock. I will get up at four o'clock, too. I will go right to Farmer Smith's farm."

When the old wolf got to Farmer Smith's farm, the three little pigs were up in the apple tree. They were picking big, red apples and putting them into their baskets.

"Good morning, little pigs," called the wolf. "Are the apples big and red?"

"Oh, yes," said the little pigs. "The apples are very good. We will get some apples for you."

The little pigs threw the apples as far from the apple tree as they could, and when the wolf ran to get the apples, the three little pigs got down from the apple tree. They ran to the little, brick house as fast as they could go.

The old wolf ran to the little, brick house, too. But the three little pigs got into the house before he got them. He jumped up and down and called to the three little pigs, "I will get you. I am going to eat three little pigs right away. I will come down your chimney right into your house. I will get you this time."

The wolf jumped and jumped. He jumped up to the top of the little, brick house.

The three little pigs in the brick house worked very fast. The first little pig made a big fire. The second little pig got a big pot and put on the fire. The third little pig put water into the pot. And the water got very, very hot.

When the wolf came down the chimney, he went right into the pot of hot water. The old wolf jumped out of the pot and ran out the door, and he never bothered the three little pigs again.

And the three little pigs lived together in the little, brick house a long, long time.

The Bear That Liked Music

Once there were two brothers who lived in the forest. One brother was always sad. His name was Peter. One brother was always happy. His name was Matti.

All day long Peter looked sad and did not say a word. Some days Peter went into the forest to cut wood.

As Peter cut wood, he looked sad and did not say a word.

Matti was always happy. He played on a guitar and sang happy songs. And when Matti played on his guitar, people had to be happy and dance.

Matti was a good worker, too. When he went to the forest to cut wood, he sang a happy song.

One cold day, Peter went into the forest to cut wood.

As he worked, Peter looked sad and did not say a word.

A bear was sleeping in his den. He heard Peter cutting wood.

"Who is making all that noise?" roared the bear. "I cannot sleep with all that noise around me."

The bear came out of his den. He saw Peter cutting wood and looking sad.

The bear was very angry.

"Get out of my forest," roared the bear.

The bear ran at Peter. Peter was afraid and ran home as fast as he could go.

It was very cold and there was no wood in the house. So Matti took his guitar and went to the forest. As he walked in the forest, he played on his guitar and sang a happy song.

Matti found the wood that Peter had been cutting.

Matti said to himself, "This is the wood that Peter was cutting to put on the fire. I must take it home because the house is cold. But first I must sing a song."

Matti played on his guitar and sang a happy song.

"Who is making all that noise?" roared the bear. "I cannot sleep with all that noise around me."

The bear came out of his den. He looked around. He saw Matti playing on his guitar and singing a happy song. The music made the bear want to dance.

The bear danced and danced. At last he sat down on the ground.

"I like your music," said the bear. "And I like to dance. You may take the wood from my forest. I will not hurt you."

Then Matti carried the wood back to the house in the forest. He made a big fire.

Matti sat by the fire and played his guitar and sang a happy song. And Peter sat by the fire and looked sad and did not say a word.

The Coldest Time of the Year

Once upon a time, the tiger said to the bear, "The winter is the coldest time of the year."

"No, no," said the bear. "The coldest time of the year is when it rains."

"No, it is the winter time," said the tiger. "Everyone knows that winter is the coldest time."

"No, it is coldest when it rains," said the bear. "Everyone knows that when you get wet, you feel cold."

The tiger and the bear saw a man in the forest. The tiger ran to the man.

"What is the coldest time of the year?" asked the tiger. "You must say that the winter is coldest or I shall eat you."

The bear ran to the man.

"What is the coldest time of the year?" asked the bear. "If you do not say that it is coldest when it rains, I shall eat you."

The man was afraid. He said, "My friends, I will tell you the time of the year that I think is the coldest, but you must not eat me."

"Tell us!" said the tiger and the bear. Each animal thought that he would eat the man if he did not say what he had been told to say.

The man said, "Would you say that the coldest time of the year is when you feel the coldest?"

"Yes," said the tiger.

"Yes," said the bear.

"It is very cold in the winter," said the man. "But your warm clothes keep you warm, if the wind does not blow on you. You get wet when it rains, but you do not feel cold if the wind does not blow on you.

"It is the wind that makes you cold in winter. It is the wind that makes you cold when it rains. I would say that the coldest time is when the wind blows and blows."

"Yes," said the tiger. "When the wind blows, I am cold."

"Yes," said the bear. "When the wind blows, I am cold. We had not thought of the wind."

The tiger did not eat the man. The bear did not eat the man. So the man went on his way.

a	be	came
about	bear	can
afraid	because	cannot
after	beds	cap
again	been	carried
Aiken-Drum	before	carry
all	behind	carrying
always	big	cat
am	biggest	catch
an	black	chair
and	blew	chicken
Andrew	blow	chickens
angry	blows	children
animal	blue	chimney
another	both	chin
any	bothered	chinny
anyone	boy	chins
anything	bread	cleaned
apple	break	cleaning
apples	breaking	clothes
apron	breaks	coat
are	brick	coconut
around	bricks	cold
as	bring	coldest
asked	brother	come
asleep	brothers	comes
at	brown	coming
ate	brownie	corn
away	brownies	could
back	but	cow
bag	butcher	cows
bake	butter	cried
baked	by	crown
baker	bye	cut
barn	cake	cutting
basket	cakes	dance
baskets	called	danced

daughter	find	happy
day	fine	hard
days	fire	has
dear	first	hat
deer	five	have
den	for	he
did	forest	head
do	forgot	hear
does	found	heard
dog	four	help
done	fox	helped
donkey	friends	hen
door	from	her
doors	full	here
down	funny	hill
dropped	garden	him
each	gave	himself
earth	get	his
eat	gingerbread	hold
eating	girl	home
elephant	give	hot
ever	go	house
every	going	houses
everyone	gold	how
everything	gone	however
eye	good	huff
eyes	got	huffed
face	grandmother	hurt
fallen	grass	I
far	green	if
farm	ground	in
farmer	grownup	into
fast	guitar	is
faster	had	it
father	hair	Jack
feel	hand	Jack's
fill	hands	joke

jump	meat	our
jumped	men	out
just	milk	oven
keep	milked	over
king	money	own
king's	monkey	pail
knew	monkeys	palace
know	more	passed
knows	morning	people
last	most	Peter
laugh	mother	picking
laughed	Mr.	pig
let	much	pigs
like	music	play
liked	must	played
lion	my	playing
little	name	please
live	named	pocket
lived	need	pot
lives	never	prettiest
long	new	pretty
look	no	princess
looked	noise	puff
looking	nose	puffed
lost	not	pull
love	now	pulling
loved	o'clock	put
loves	of	putting
made	off	queen
make	oh	rabbit
makes	old	rabbits
making	on	rain
man	once	rains
many	one	ran
Matti	only	red
may	opened	rich
me	or	right

ring	someone	tiger
road	something	time
roared	song	times
room	songs	tired
round	soon	to
run	started	together
running	stick	told
sad	sticks	too
said	stone	took
sang	stopped	top
sat	store	town
saw	straw	tree
say	street	turnips
scissors	string	two
second	sun	under
see	table	up
seen	take	upon
sewed	talking	us
shall	tell	very
she	telling	walk
should	thank	walked
show	that	want
showed	the	wanted
silly	their	wanting
sing	them	wants
singing	then	warm
sit	there	was
six	they	water
sleep	things	way
sleeping	think	we
smell	thinking	went
Smith	third	were
Smith's	this	wet
snow	those	what
so	thought	when
soldiers	three	where
some	threw	white

who   wolf   working
why   woman   works
wife   women   would
will   wood   year
wind   woods   yellow
windows   word   yes
winter   work   you
wish   worked   your
with   worker